The original pictures for BAYBERRY BLUFF were printed from cardboard cuts. Cardboard cuts are similar to woodcuts except that the designs are cut into thick cardboard with single-edged razor blades instead of in wood with woodcutting tools. The cuts are printed on the artist's own small printing press, then the prints are cut apart to create the different colors for each picture in the book and prepared for the printer. The printer photographs the artwork and transfers it to metal printing plates so that the book can be printed on a large commercial press.

Many thanks to Sue Smith—and most especially to Deborah Dunham and Ellen Wineberg for their help and their enthusiasm.

WORDS AND PICTURES BY
❀ **BLAIR LENT** ❀

BAYBERRY BLUFF

HOUGHTON MIFFLIN COMPANY BOSTON 1987

Library of Congress Number 86-27232
ISBN 0-395-35384-X

Printed in the United States of America

H 10 9 8 7 6 5 4 3 2 1

at last, for Sue

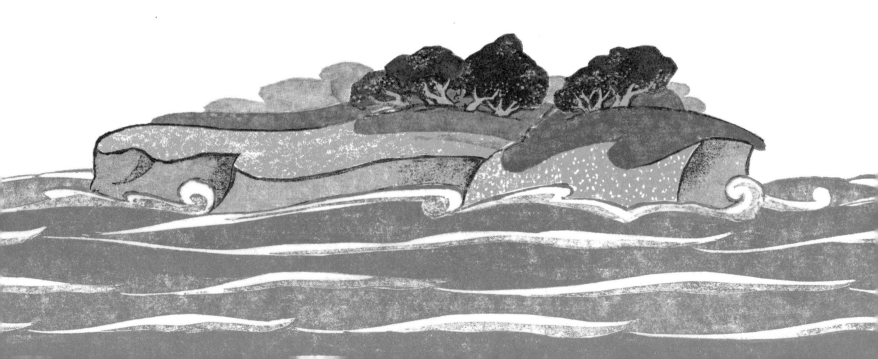

Summer after summer
the Mermaid chugged across the bay,

across the bay to an island,

an island where bayberries grow.

The passengers from the steamboat Mermaid
gathered on a bluff above the sea.
Shaded by parasols, they enjoyed the view.

One summer,
visitors to the island wanted to stay overnight;
so they pitched tiny tents in a circle;

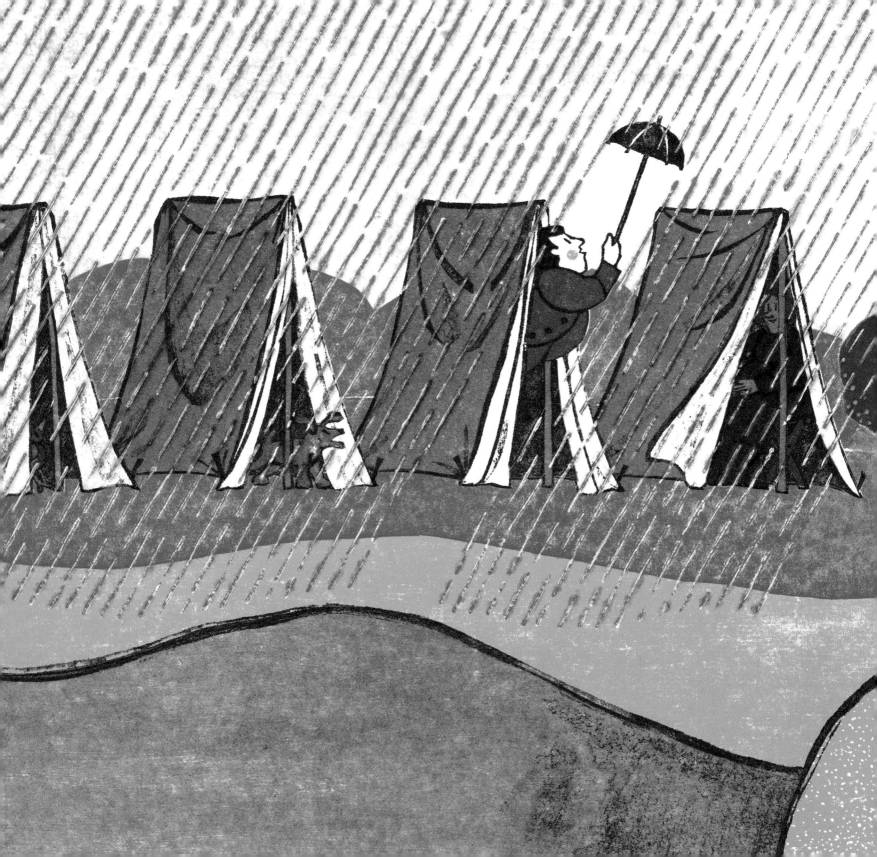

and they pitched tiny tents in rows.

The visitors loved the island.
They wanted to stay for a week or two;
so they stretched canvas over
big wooden frames.

The big tents were decorated,
sometimes with seashells, flowers and leaves,
sometimes with animals cut from cloth.

Summers went by.

People didn't want to leave the island at all.

Now there are buildings in a circle
and houses in rows.
There is a village on the island . . .

a village called Bayberry Bluff.

About the Story

The village of Bayberry Bluff exists only in this book but the story of how Bayberry Bluff became a village is influenced by fact.

There is a village called Oak Bluffs on Martha's Vineyard, an island off the coast of Massachusetts, where Blair Lent has visited many times. Oak Bluffs is one of many villages on Martha's Vineyard, a larger island than the one in the book, and Oak Bluffs is unique. During the early part of the nineteenth century Oak Bluffs

was a summer tenting ground; but by the end of the century all the tents had evolved into little brightly painted and elaborately decorated houses very similar to the houses in the book. Some other American villages, Alton Bay, New Hampshire, and Asbury Park and Ocean City, both in New Jersey, have similar histories.

Oak Bluffs still looks the same as it did a long time ago. You can go there and find animal and flower motifs in the wooden ornamental work that decorate the houses. Many of these designs were influenced by earlier tent decorations, just as in this story.